A Hero for Quale
The Watcher Fairies

S. A. Sutton

Strategic Book Group

Strategic Book Group
P.O. Box 333
Durham CT 06422
www.StrategicBookClub.com

ISBN: 978-1-60976-779-2

Printed in the United States of America

Book Design: Suzanne Kelly

I dedicate this book to all of those who helped me make this book. And to my family who loved the first book, and wanted to have the second.

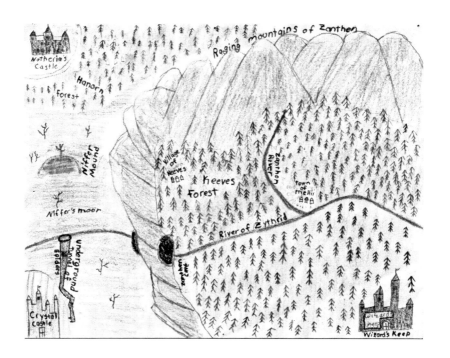

Raging mountains of Zanthen

Natheria's Castle

Hanorn forest

Niffer Mound

Niffer's moor

Village of Keeves

Keeves Forest

Zanthen River

Town of Mellis

River of Zythrid

Zanthen Cave

underground tunnel to spiders

Crystal Castle

Wizard's Keep

Table of Contents

Queen

"My queen, three days ago a young-looking boy happened upon my shop in the town of Mellii. He was dressed in strange clothes," said a man who was kneeling on one knee in front of a throne, which was clouded in shadow. The said man looked up to see if there was any reaction from his tale.

"So he has come at last has he? Well he won't be around much longer to cause me any problems." There was a slight movement from within the shadow, and a young-looking woman appeared—long, blonde wavy hair, eyes so blue they were like ice. If any man should look upon those eyes, they would freeze where they stood.

Queen Natheria was her name and she ruled Quale, and she was not going to allow the threat that came to ruin her plans. The queen smirked as she walked down the stairs in slow and preppy movements. As she reached the bottom, she reached out and touched the cheek of the man in front of her.

"My dear spy, you have been very loyal to me this day. For this you shall be rewarded."

"My queen, how could I not obey you? I serve you and only you." Sweat was beginning to streak down his neck in fear.

"That's right, my dear spy. Only me." *SLAP.* The man fell over on his side holding his cheek, his eyes open in fear.

"I don't want you to just bring me news, Banner! WHY didn't you kill him then and there?" A red gleam surrounded the queen as she awaited the answer from the sniveling merchant spy.

"Yo Ashton, Your Highness, he stopped me. One of my objects disappeared and I tried to blame him and I yelled for him to be hung, but Yo Ashton forbade it . . ." *SLAP.* "Agh!" Banner cried out once again, holding his other cheek.

"I DO NOT WANT EXUSES! You go back there and find that BRAT and kill him or it will be *you* who shall face my wrath."

"Y . . . Yes, my queen, right away." Banner pulled himself up and started running for the door.

"Oh and Banner . . .," the fat man in question turned, "keep up the good work." Banner flinched as he ran.

"Misstresss?" a hissy, sandpapered voice came from behind the throne. The queen stood where she was not acknowledging the person behind her.

"You were caught by that disgusting wizard; how dare you even come here." She slowly turned and faced a rugged creature. "Why have you come back?"

"I came because you need me, queeny; you need Zonks. Zonks did what queeny wanted—got rid of prince." Zonks took a limply step forward.

"Oh you did, did you? Well then tell me why my merchant spy in Mellii came to me and told me of a strange boy wearing strange clothes." The red glowing surrounding her began to hum and move in fluid ways.

"Boy die, boy die, I saw it with my eyes, queeny. He fell from carriage screaming. He did, he did." He howled, covering his face with his hands. He fell forward onto his knees, the chain from his collar rattling.

"Oh be quiet. Yes I have thought about it and you are perfect. That stupid wizard thinks he destroyed you and yet here you are. Yes, it will be perfect, Zonks," his fingers spread open and two beady eyes looked from within, "if Banner fails in destroying that child, then you can eat them both, the brat and Banner." Zonks removed his hands and grinned a great wide grin showing all his teeth. Drool appeared streaming out at the mere thought of it.

"Mmm," she said, tapping her chin. She thought about her attack on the child only ten minutes before Banner arrived. Yes, she already knew the chosen one was here, by better and more reliable spies than Banner. Her plan would have worked if it had not been for that wizard. How had he found the child so fast? It made no difference though; she knew she would win in the end.

A Hair Brush?

A sixteen-year-old boy with white-gold hair running down his back was sitting in a black leather chair reading a novel. His silver eyes were zigzagging back and forth from one side of the book to the other.

The boy's name was Whisper Shade. He lived in an ancient mansion that was four stories high and had over twenty rooms. But even with all the spacious room, he was not alone. With him were two others, one other boy and a girl.

The other boy looked about seventeen with short, flaming red hair that reached his shoulders and amber eyes that were always packed with mischief. His name was Wolly Sims.

The girl was a princess in every way. Looking a mere ten years with crystal fine, ebony strands that reached her waist and ice blue eyes that had the stars dancing within. Crystal Shade was her name. For two hours she walked down the hall toward the library to find her long lost brother. Crystal knew that Whisper loved to read and if he was missing, the library was the first place to look.

Crystal slowly opened the library door making sure that no noise of any kind came from it. Her eyes darted around the room until they came to a halt on Whisper's bent form. A sudden flash of light drew her gaze form her brother and a small gasp forced its way through her cherry fine lips. For up on the top of one of the book shelves, was the most beautiful thing Crystal had ever seen. A monster in her chest rose up and screeched, "I must have it!"

Whisper was engrossed with a novel he held so gently in his hands. It was the first one off the shelf that he had not read yet. The book was hiding, moving around, and becoming a challenge for Whisper. But he had won in the end. He had out-smarted the book and now he had his prize.

SMASH! Whisper looked up and what he saw made him raise an eyebrow. For there on floor rubbing her hurt bum was Crystal.

"Can you please make more racket? I don't think Wolly heard you," he said with a placid face.

"Shut up, Whisper," she snarled at him. Then—as if a switch was flipped—she was once again a bubbly ten-year-old. She hopped up and jutted out her left hand, nearly hitting Whisper in the face.

"Look at what I found, Whisper. It was up top of that bookshelf over there, just floating there. I could hear it talking, Whisper. It said come and get me if you can, little girl. I knew that I had to make it mine."

Hovering there inches from his face was the most sparkling hair brush he had ever seen. *BAM!* Whisper and Crystal turned and saw Wolly run into the room, and then skid to a stop when he had noticed them.

"Hey princess, what you got there? Ah, so you're the one making all of the racket," he said as he reached up and caught one of the dangling candles he had hit with head as he ran into the room.

"It's a magical hair brush, Wolly. It's got diamonds and rubies and pearls in it. All made for a lovely princess. I saw it floating up top of that bookcase over there. It even talked to me, didn't it Whisper?" She turned and glanced down at Whisper only to see that he had gone back to reading the squirming novel.

"Whisper!" screeched Crystal.

"What? Yes it did. So what, leave me alone," he murmured, not looking up. Wolly watched the exchanged with humor living in his eyes. Then he got a glint in his eyes that just spoke of mischief.

He started to scoot his way over to Whisper trying to be inconspicuous to the quarreling siblings. Wolly smiled a sinister smile as he got in range of his target. He then launched forward as if his heels were on fire, and knocked the squirming novel out of Whisper's hands. The book hopped up and immediately ran off.

"Wolly, do you know how long it took to me to finally catch that book?" Whisper screamed. His silver eyes had the look of hardened stone as they glared at the now-laughing red head. If looks could kill, Wolly would be dead.

"Is it safe to come down now?" a musical voice asked. Both boys looked up and saw Crystal hovering a few feet above them, her blue hue-colored wings patted up and down.

"Yes, Crystal, it is. I'm sorry for scaring you." It was just then that Whisper noticed his wings were out as well. He took a deep breath, let it out, and folded his violet wings.

Wolly was still snickering when all three pairs of pointed ears twitched as they heard a clicking sound. As one, they all looked down as the floor opened up to reveal a gigantic slide.

All three looked at one another with blank looks, and then a smile crawled up simultaneously. Eyes glazing with mischief, all three jumped. Night had come and it was time to play in human children's dreams.

Understanding

BAM! All three hit the hard floor.

"What the . . .?" Wolly said as he rubbed his head, for he had been planning to go head first this time.

"What happened? Why did it close?" asked Whisper.

"Ahh good, I got here just in time . . ." All three turned to see the high wizard's "eye" looking at them. Crystal got up off the floor and walked over to the door and opened it. Whisper and Wolly followed her.

As one, they flew out and landed on a small table. Darius walked over and sat down in a large chair. He looked at the fairies, who were no bigger than his pinky finger.

"Watcher Fairies, I have a request to ask of you." Whisper flew up and landed on his shoulder.

"What kind of request, High Wizard?"

"As you all know, Queen Natheria is spreading her poison to the far reaches of Quale. Of course you also know of the chosen one."

"Of course," they said simultaneously.

"A cohort of mine by the name of Zenchen went to the world of humans and found the chosen one." The reaction was instantaneous.

"The chosen one, are you sure?" said Wolly.

"They really found him; oh my, this is wonderful!" gasped Crystal.

"He *did* bring him here, didn't he?" the last was said by Whisper, his eyes were filled with concern and wonder.

"Yes he did," Darius said and all three fairies started to dance around in a circle.

"But," Darius said, his voice raised a small fraction, "one of the queen's subordinates was on the carriage. Zenchen knew nothing of this, nor did I." The fairies hissed a nasty sound.

"He made the boy fall from the carriage with the intention of killing him," Crystal gasped and tears brimmed in her eyes.

"He did not; but instead he was found and healed by the Ashton family. The child recovered his necklace with my help, and with it had many memories resurface. It was too much for him and he went into a deep sleep afterwards." Darius paused in his telling so the fairies could absorb it.

"While in this deep sleep the queen made her move." Whisper and Wolly's body turned a nasty shade of red as they grew angry. Crystal's turned white, fearing the worst.

"She cast a burning spell on him hoping to kill his heart. I fought it off but it weakened me, for she was very persistent. Afterwards, the most miraculous thing happened; Princess Arria sent him her energy." Crystal sighed and batted her eyelashes while the boys rolled their eyes, but they had a smile.

"That is what brings me here. We need your help to keep him safe with your fairy magic. The queen cannot fight off your magic, for she believes that you are all gone. Will you help us?" The three watcher fairies turned and looked at one another, nodded, and turned back to Darius who had a smile on his face.

"We will," they said simultaneously.

New Allies

Darius returned to the Ashton Inn, which was owned by Yo and Kendal Ashton, with a loud *POP* and a quick flash. He could see that Derek, the boy he sent for from another world, was still on the couch asleep or unconscious; he did not know which. Kadunks, who was the half-cat son of Yo and Kendal, was lying on a small pallet on the floor near Derek fast asleep. Yo, Kendal, Yo's twin Yang, and Zenchen were all in the kitchen waiting for the high wizard to return.

"What have you found?" asked Yo, standing up. The others looked at Darius awaiting the answer. Darius chuckled for a moment then lifted his hand.

"It is not what I have found, but who I brought." He made a "come here" motion. They all waited but nothing happened.

"Uhh, Darius, what exactly did you bring?" asked Zenchen, looking around trying to spot whatever it was. Darius was confused for a moment, and then was frantically looking for the fairies. Not seeing them, he went into a state of momentary panic.

Darius stopped as he heard a giggle emerging from the living room. He then slapped his forehead.

"Of course," he said. He left the kitchen with the others right behind him. They headed for the living room. Darius stopped and smiled and looked at the others who were bewildered as to why he was smiling. Darius moved into the room and stood by the door with the others.

"Meet the watcher fairies," he said as he pointed to the couch.

Kadunks was having a great dream, when all of the sudden he felt something brush past his nose. Not just once but several times. He slowly opened his eyes and there in front of him standing on his chest was a tiny fairy. He had red hair, brown leather clothes, and gold wings. Kadunks blinked his eyes for a moment as if to see if it was really there.

"Hiya," the fairy said.

Kadunks giggled. "Hi, my name Kadunks, what's yours?"

"Nice to meet you, Kadunks, the name's Wolly, pleasure." Wolly made a salute of the hand. Kadunks saw some movement behind Wolly and made his eyes focus. He saw Darius smiling and his mom and dad, his uncle, and the other dude, standing there with shocked looks on their faces.

"W-Watcher F-Fairies?" yelled Zenchen; the others flinched at the high noise.

"Yes."

"But . . . but I thought they all moved on and that there were none left here?" stuttered Zenchen as he sat down not believing his eyes.

"All but these three. I found them in the Horan Forest one morning a few years back—when the king still ruled this land—hiding under a mushroom. I told them of my castle and that I would help them. They promised to return the favor later on and so, viola!" Darius turned back and looked at Derek; the other two fairies were sitting on his chest watching him sleep. Darius smiled, for he knew now that he made the right choice.

Derek slowly opened his eyes and groaned because of the light; he blinked a bit to adjust them. He rubbed his eyes to get the sleep out of them and slowly sat up. "Whoa!" Derek heard, and he felt something fall into his lap. He looked down and saw a fairy upside down and tangled up in the covers. He watched as the fairy tugged his head from underneath the cover, his hair all in disarray. Derek snickered and the fairy glared at him, which made him snicker even more until he was flat out laughing. His sudden outburst of laughter must have caught on because the fairy was rolling around in his lap laughing as well. The fairy had white hair with silver eyes and violet wings.

"Hello, my name is Whisper Shade and I'm a watcher fairy. There are two more of us here and we are here to protect you from the evil queen from now on," Whisper said with a little bow.

"Where are the others?" Derek asked, looking around to see if he could spot them. Whisper jumped up and flew down to where Kadunks lay, and on the boy's legs sat two other fairies.

"The one with red hair is Wolly Sims," said Whisper.

"Howdy," said Wolly with a mock salute. Whisper rolled his eyes and turned to the girl.

"This is our little sister; her name is Crystal Shade," said Whisper.

"Hello, it's nice to meet you," Crystal said with a small smile and a curtsy, her body turning a little pink in color. She had blue wings that pattered, ice blue eyes that were round and soft, and her hair was a beautifully shade of ebony.

"Ah good, you're awake." Derek looked up and saw Darius flanked by Yo and Yang. Yo went over to Kadunks and smiled at the watcher fairies and his son.

"Kadunks you need to get up and get dressed; we are leaving in a little while." Kadunks got up and went to do what his father said.

"Leaving? Where are we going?" asked Derek as he too started to get up.

"Yes, we have a lot of ground to cover in order to get to the princess," Darius said.

"Not to mention kicking the queen off her high horse," said Yang, his back against the wall and his arms crossed. Darius then laid a small map on the table.

Onward

"Here we are," Darius said as he pointed to a small dot with the word Mellii next to it. "Now, Mellii is right at the junction of two rivers—the Zythrid River and the Zanthon River. I would say the fastest route is to cross Zanthon, and then follow the Zythrid River to the mountains. Now I know for a fact there is a cave there where the river flows into. We may have to build a raft and let the river carry us down it." Darius looked up to the group, Yo and Yang were nodding their heads in agreement.

"What is this?" Derek was pointing to a spot on the map that read: The Underground Tunnel of Spiders.

"That is exactly what it means. The guardian put the spiders in there to deter people from taking some unknown treasure from within. Many men went in to find that treasure; none came out alive save one, and he was the one to tell everyone about the tunnel."

"Uh, Darius, how big are the spiders?" asked Derek, little paler in the face.

"They are the size of an average man," Darius said with utmost seriousness.

"Darius, talking about spiders, there is a rumor going around that the princess has a guardian spider that the queen could not destroy," said Zenchen with curiosity.

"That, I am afraid, is no rumor. I have seen it with my own eyes. The beast is the height of fourteen men, fiery red eyes, and his exoskeleton is as white as snow. He has powers I do not know of, but I do know he withheld the queen and made a run for it toward the tunnel of spiders. Where do you think the name came from, eh?" Everyone was silent for few minutes as they tried to picture the creature within their minds. Darius shook his head out of the daze.

"Well enough of that; we need to head out as soon as it hits dusk. That way, no one will know we have left until the middle of tomorrow afternoon." Everybody nodded as they went around for last-minute packing. When dusk came, Yo locked the inn and put up the closed sign. Darius, in lead, headed off for the gates of Mellii; Zenchen was behind him with Yang at his side. Derek came next in line walking beside Kadunks, who had two out of three fairies hitching a ride on his shoulders. The third, Whisper, was on Derek's shoulder. Yo and Kendal brought up the rear.

When the first break came, Derek flopped down on the ground with a groan, lying on his back with one arm hung over his eyes.

"Ha ha, you can't be that tuckered, Derek?" asked Yo. Derek turned and glared at him, which brought on more chuckles not only from Yo, but from everyone.

"It's not funny; the most I've ever done was in PE and that was hard enough," Derek said with a smile he couldn't hold back.

"What's pee ee?" asked Kadunks.

"It's PE. It stands for physical education. It's where grownups make you run and do a lot of exercises to keep your body fit," Derek explained to everyone.

"Ohh, kinda like what Daddy and Uncle Yang do with their bows."

"It's Uncle Yang and Daddy, sweetie, but yes, it sounds like it," said Kendal.

The group got up and set off again. Two hours later they had arrived at the river. Derek's eyes went wide; the river was huge. It was almost as big as the Mississippi. Darius was busy looking around left to right, right to left.

"Are we going to build a raft to get across?" asked Derek.

"We might just have to. I know this river has a bridge but it's old. I don't know if it can hold us up. Not many people come this way anymore," answered Darius.

"Darius, if I may?" The wizard turned to see Kendal. "My people have built a new bridge not far from here and it is new. They have always used the path at night to hunt in the forest," she said as she pointed to the right. "It is not very far from here, maybe ten miles at the most."

Darius nodded his head and looked at the others. "Do we all agree that the road we take is the bridge

people have against humans," Kendal said with a bit of sadness and loathing, her tail slashing back and forth.

"I know, but we need them Kendal," Then he bowed his head and went off to set up his tent. Yo came up behind Kendal and hugged her.

"It will be fine. I will be by your side the whole time as will our son, along with everyone else, not that we have a choice, but you know what I mean," Yo said, then smiled as a small laugh came from his wife. Derek, Kadunks, Zenchen, and Yang all came back into the camp, all of them loaded down with firewood.

A short time later, the twins went out and returned with food. They all ate, and then settled down for the night. As Derek was falling asleep, he could hear the forest all around them start to sing its nightly song.

Derek woke to Zenchen gently shaking his shoulder. The group packed up and set out once again. They crossed the bridge but not before Yang went over it once and came back to ensure the safety of the bridge. Once everything was in order, the group set out once more. Derek found that they had walked for nearly half the day. He was caring Kadunks on his back, for the little one's feet hurt him and he was not used to walking very far.

"We're not far from the village, Darius, but I should warn you a few meters from here are the outposts and the start of Keeve's territory. They have guards patrolling all around these parts so be careful," advised Kendal. Everyone nodded, readjusted their packs, and moved on. As they walked their way into nightfall, Derek had this shaky feeling that he was being watched and as he looked at the others, it seemed they shared his feeling. No one had said anything since Kendal gave her words a while back. Kadunks had tried to make conversation with Derek but his father hushed him. After that, no one said anything.

Then suddenly an arrow shot right next to Derek's head, and embedded itself in a nearby tree. What happened then was so fast Derek could not see. The Ashton twins whipped out their bows, poised and ready. Zenchen and Kendal pulled out long swords and had stepped into a defensive stance.

Even Kadunks had his small dagger out and had his back against Derek's. On impulse, Derek had also pulled out his small dagger, but unlike the others who looked like they knew what they were doing, he was shaking with fear—fear of dying and the fear of not using the dagger right.

"Who are you and why are you in our forest?" said a gruff voice off to the right.

"We are no enemy of yours; we only seek the village of Keeve for sanction along with their help," said Darius, his staff in both hands.

"We do not help humans, go away."

"Wait, I am Keeve and I wish to enter my village in hopes to see my loved ones," said Kendal.

"Wait. No, you cannot be, Kendal Grash, the one who left the village for some *human*?" the voice spat.

"It was not because of some human; he is my mate and the father of my child. You know the rules of the village; the wife goes where her mate leads. Who am I to do any different?" Kendal said with her head slightly tilted upward. There was silence for a few moments, then some rustles from the trees gave way to a tall, humanoid cat-man. He was orange and yellow by color, with bright green eyes that shown in the moonlight.

"Fine, you may enter but know this; if you are liars or servants of that hag, you will be killed," said the Keeve guard. He turned and started in toward the forest, the others following taking their lead. Kendal was the first of the camp to move forward.

"Why was he so mean to you, Kendal?" asked Derek in a whisper. Everyone looked to her for an answer. Yo looked to the ground for moment but then he held his head high, and gave Kendal a loving smile. Kadunks was looking at his mother and father with curiosity and worry, for he had never seen his parents this way before.

"I was banished a long time ago. I was banished because I fell in love with a human male. That is forbidden in my land. My family turned their backs on me, but they gave me one chance to regain my position in the tribe. They wanted me to forget my love, but I knew in my heart that he was the one for me so I declined. Since then I have been dead to them, but I do not care; I love my family and if I had a chance to do it again I would," Kendal said with a glimmer of tears in her eyes as she looked at her son and husband. Yo reached over and took her hand and smiled, then leaned over and kissed her. Tears were in his eyes too Derek noticed.

To him that was sad—losing your family just because you fell in love with someone your parents didn't like. He shook his head and looked over to his right shoulder and saw Whisper perched there. He noted that Whisper had become a light shade of blue. Derek looked over to Kadunks and noticed the other fairies were the same color.

"Whisper, why are you and the others blue?" he asked, looking back to the fairy.

"Oh, well we fairies are so small that we can only hold one emotion at a time. The reason we are blue is because we are sad. Kendal's story left us sad," Whisper said. Crystal and Wolly both nodded their heads and Derek noticed that when he spoke to them their color started to become normal again.

"I need you to wait here while I go let the counsel know that you are here," spoke the Keeve guard, and then he turned and was gone within the trees. His troop stayed and formed a line in front of Derek and the group.

"Mommy, am I going to meet my grandma and grandpa from your side now?" asked Kadunks, his eyes wide with excitement.

"Well, maybe sweetie, I do hope so," said Kendal as she sat down and drew her son into her lap. Yo sat beside her and started to play with her hair to calm her down. Zenchen and Yang sat down in a huddle talking about past times. Darius just kept standing, but was looking up at the stars.

Whisper, Crystal, and Wolly had jumped down and now stood in circle just talking and Wolly began to move and make funny jokes to make the other two laugh. Derek sat down too, but he sat and just watched the fairies do their thing.

An hour had passed since the guard had left and so Kendal and her son were softly dozing while leaning on an alert. Yo, Zenchen, and Yang had joined up with Darius and now the four were just gazing at the stars. The fairies flew over to Derek and had laid beside him on leaves and fallen asleep. Derek too was fighting sleep, as his eyes kept falling. Just when he thought he could not hold it any longer there was rustling in the bushes behind the line of guards. Those asleep were jerked awake and joined the others. The Keeve guard had returned.

"The elders have agreed to see you. Now if you will follow me," he said as he started walking again. Everyone followed him until he came to a huge tree. He stopped in front of it then turned to see if everyone was there, then nodded. The guard turned his attention to the tree once more and tapped a knob three times.

A soft humming sound appeared, and then a crunching sound took its place as the trees separated to reveal a village within. The village was small with little grass huts. There was a gathering of Keeves at the entrance who were, from what Derek saw, crying.

"Ah!" an old woman had cried before she started to run toward the group. Kendal had then ran forward and met the old woman in a ground-crashing hug. There was lot of crying and squeals from the rest of the Keeves; by then they had run up and joined in with the hugging.

"Who is that, Daddy?" asked Kadunks, his tail tucked between his legs, for he was worried his mother might be hurt.

"That is your grandmother, Kadunks, and all the other girls around her are your aunts and cousins," said Yo, who took his hand and gently led Kadunks to the squealing party. Derek smiled, knowing it would be a great reunion.

What!

Derek felt a little out of place when he watched Kendal with her family. At first it was happiness, but soon it turned to sadness, for he was remembering his dad. A small gust of wind blew on Derek's face and he felt a coolness on his cheeks. He reached up with his hands and found that he was crying. He immediately wiped them away but soon found that he could not stop.

"Derek?" Derek turned to see Darius, Yang, and Zenchen standing behind him. The fairies were on each one of their shoulders. It was Darius who had called him, and as soon as he had turned around, they saw the tears. Darius stepped forward and placed Derek in a hug, holding him as tears rolled down his cheeks. Derek needed nothing else, for that was the last straw; he could not hold it in any longer. He cried. He cried for his father, he cried for his mother, and he cried for everything that had happened to him so far.

Derek heard sweet words come from the wizard and the other two men standing near. After what seemed to be an eternity, he finally stopped.

"M'sorry," he mumbled, a little embarrassed by what had just occurred. He could not believe that he had just cried in front of them. That was just not how it went down with guys. But he felt so much better; he could not argue with that.

"There is no need to apologize, Derek. What just happened was natural. Even grown men like myself have been known to cry every once in a while." Darius smiled as he patted Derek's back.

"I don't know what came over me; one minute I was fine and the next I was crying," Derek said.

"All I do know is that when I saw Kendal and her family smiling and crying I thought of my dad, and how worried he must be right now. After my mom died, I was the only thing holding him down. He told me that without me being there, he would not know what to do with himself any more. I was like his lifeline and now that I am here and not there . . ." Derek once again swiped tears from his face as he thought of the worst for his father.

"Derek, it is okay. I told your father I was coming to get you." Derek jerked around to look at Zenchen.

"What?"

"You don't know do you?" Zenchen asked, looking from Derek to Darius.

"Know what? You told my dad? What did he say in return?" Derek was frantic trying to find out.

"Derek, settle down; I will explain everything. What Zenchen did by telling your father where you were going was right by him. For you see, your father knows about Quale." Derek just looked at Darius, not saying anything; he just sat down on the ground blinking.

"Your father was a hard-working young man. He had morals and was kind and just. For these reasons your mother sought him out. At first, she was hesitant, but soon became enthralled with your father. It was not long after they met that they fell in love. It was hard for her to keep away from him. Her father was very worried that she was getting into something that was a little bit more that she could handle. But alas, she did not listen." Darius paused and sat down near Derek, Zenchen, and Yang also. Derek heard some rattling noise and looked up to see everyone was listening to the tail that Darius was telling.

"Her father soon realized that it was her destiny to be with this man. Soon they came for his permission to get married; he did not stand in their way. They were very happy. The father then went back to his home and was content that his daughter was in good hands. A few months later, your mother got a hold of her father and told him that she was pregnant." Derek looked at Darius smiling a bit, knowing it was him that she was carrying.

"All three were ecstatic over the news. Then the tragedy happened; your mother went into labor. It seemed like any ordinary one, but things change. Yes they change, and very quickly. She was very tired; it was twenty hours into the labor and she simply had no energy left. The doctors could not find out what was wrong until it was too late. They had found that she was bleeding internally and it had been happening throughout her labor." Derek noticed that the wizard's eyes were getting misty and he looked as if he was reliving everything he told.

"The doctors wheeled her out saying they had to take the baby before it was too late. That was the last time your father and her father saw her alive. After they delivered you, she died." A small tear ran down Darius's face, but he did not wipe it away; he was too into what he was saying to care.

"Your father lost it. He started to scream and pound his fist upon the walls in blind sorrow. Soon he just huddled in the floor crying and saying that there was nothing worth living for anymore. But her father went over and picked him up and shook him hard." Derek's eyes went wide hearing this.

"As he held onto his son-in-law, he told him that he had a perfectly healthy son in there waiting for him, and that son was a part of her too. So he could not give up, and he did not. As soon as he had seen you, he shed different tears—tears of joy." Darius looked upon Derek with a new look in his eyes that Derek had seen only once before, and that was when the wizard had given him back his necklace. Derek was confused by this look, but he was not afraid of it.

"You see, Derek, the reason your father knows of Quale is because your mother was from here."

"What?" Derek asked, his eyes wide with shock that that was even possible.

"Yes, she was from here and not only that Derek . . ." Darius got up and motioned for Derek to do the same. Once he was standing, Darius placed his hands on Derek's shoulders. "She was my daughter."

Festival

"Wait what? Derek is your grandson?" asked Zenchen as he looked from Derek to Darius.

"Yes, but I did not want this knowledge to be out in the open. But in this case, I felt it was the right time to tell Derek that he does indeed have family here." Darius smiled a loving smile to Derek. Derek wondered if he should feel weird by having a grandfather that looked like he was no older than himself, but as he searched his feelings in the matter, all he felt now was love. Love for this man who was indeed his grandfather. Derek suddenly felt like shouting and crying and laughing all at once. It was like a euphoria he had never felt before.

He had a part of his mother with him, a part that he could touch, talk to, and love. Derek then hugged his new-found grandfather. But in the excitement of their bouncing embrace, he did it a little too hard, as both went tumbling to the ground.

"Oh I'm sorry, Grandpa; I was just going to hug you," Derek said as he started to get off him. But Darius held tight, preventing the movement.

"Is that so, young man? Well it seems that since you want to send old men to the ground, then you shall be punished." Derek had a look of fear in his eyes for a brief second, thinking he had stepped over some line that had to do with grandparents. But that thought left his mind as he was suddenly wiggling and laughing as his grandfather tickled him. Everyone around then started to laugh as well. It was indeed a great day for family reunions.

Later on that night, Derek saw that the Keeve women had arranged some kind of banquet with a lot of fresh food. He also noticed the men had dragged in big piles of wood and formed them into a large, wooden tee pee in the center of a circle of rocks. Derek was wondering what exactly was going on when he saw a group of Keeve women and men walk past in wildly colored costumes. Derek suddenly thought of an Indian tribe with similar dress that he had seen in one of his history books back at school.

He noticed his grandfather was walking toward him with the three fairies riding on his shoulders.

"Hello, my grandson. I love saying that now," he said with a smile that lit up his eyes. "I see you have noticed the preparations for the festival tonight."

"Festival?" Derek asked.

"Yes, a festival for Kendal and her new family. You see for every Keeve woman, there is a dance the tribe does to ensure the safety of the baby when it is born. They dress the child in a light silk gown made from the silk worms near the river. They then lay it on a bed made of grass and dance around it to wish it many good days to follow," Darius said.

"But wait, Kadunks is five; how is that going to work?" Derek wondered.

"Ah, he is going to participate in the dance along with his mother and her family. You will enjoy it," Darius said as he got up to move.

"Wait, we will do a dance as well," said Wolly as he looked at the other two, who nodded their heads in agreement.

"You are? Well won't that be a sight to see. Not many have seen a dance of the watcher fairies. I myself have never seen such a wondrous event." Darius walked away just as two Keeve men approached him. Derek saw that they had talked for a while and it seemed the men were excited about something. He saw Darius nod his head and look back at him and smile. Derek tilted his head, wondering what that was about.

As the day grew darker, the Keeve people grew more anxious over the upcoming dance. He saw the village elder come up and stand in front of the wooden tee pee. That was when Derek noticed that all of the people had gathered around.

"This year's dance of good fortune for a newborn babe will be done differently. This year, we are blessed to have with us the last three watcher fairies and they have agreed to dance for us on this glorious night. Now light the grand fire and let the dance begin." The elder smiled and waved to the torch men.

Everyone yelled and the torches set ablaze the wooden pile. Derek watched as the watcher fairies came into view. All three wore a white gown; they shimmered in the light of the fire. Whisper and Wolly's gown reminded Derek of something the old Roman Empire used to wear, while Crystal's made her look like a glistening princess. Derek then saw Kadunks and his mother Kendal sitting nearby, wearing the same thing but only bigger.

Then the music flared up first with the drums, then the flutes, and then he saw the most amazing thing ever—Whisper and Wolly started to dance around Crystal while she stood still. Their colors started flaring from blue, red, green, yellow, purple, pink, white, black, silver, and gold. Soon they took to the air, flying around each other in circles. Then they zapped around the bonfire in the middle, going faster and faster till you saw nothing but colors. It was like seeing a rainbow in the flesh, dancing around the fire. Derek did not know who it was but one fairy stopped near him and started to spin right there. The others were doing the same thing. Derek saw there was a small line of light that connected the three, making it look like a triangle in the sky. That was when he heard it, a small musical chant being sung. In perfect sync with each other, the fairies moved once again, slowly moving in toward the fire while dancing around and moving their bodies in liquid waves just like the fire. Their colors were blasting in sync with their movements. It was truly beautiful. A fairy stopped and moved to the ground; the colors the fairy was producing grew until it made a large version of the fairy on the ground, and it started to dance with arms flaring up in the air, and the bodies moving with the beat of the drums. The other two landed and did the same thing and joined in with the mystical dance; the chanting grew faster now. Then a sudden flash of light appeared and engulfed everyone.

Then nothing, it was over. The fairies had ended their dance with one leg out and their backs bent backward some, arms hanging down, and their heads kicked back as well. The Keeve village went in an uproar of clapping and yells, Derek being one of them. He could not believe he had just seen something that wonderful before. It was like seeing a belly dancer along with a strobe light at the same time, only ten times better.

Derek ran over to his grandfather who was standing near the fairies. "That was the most amazing thing I have ever seen," he said with a huge grin on his face, and his eyes filled with wonder.

"Thank you, Derek, that pleases us that you liked it. We were worried we might not be able to make the doppelgangers because we have not done the dance in such a long time. But as you saw, we did quite well," said Whisper, smiling to the others.

Kendal came over with Kadunks and Yo. "Thank you, Watcher Fairies, for such a wondrous dance. It filled me with joy and amazement watching you. Thank you again for such a beautiful sight. But for now it is getting late and this little one needs to go to bed," said Kendal.

She smiled as Kadunks rubbed his eyes and said, "I'm not sleepy, Momma." Yo laughed, picked up their son, and walked off to their tent.

"Yes, it is time to settle in. Come this way, Derek; you will stay with me this night," Darius said as he too walked off. Derek followed, looking forward to a night of colorful dreams.

34

Watcher Fairies

Everyone woke the next morning and gathered around to make preparations for the next stop the group would make. Derek was sticking close to his grandfather, wanting to be near him. Darius would smile at him and give him nods during these times, telling him it was okay for him to do this. Kadunks and the fairies were hopping about in excitement about Derek being Darius's grandson. With the festival last night, everyone forgot about it until this morning.

"What did the elder mean last night about you guys being the last three fairies here?" asked Derek.

"The watcher fairies have been in this realm for a long time—hundreds of years—so they finally decided to go home. When the other watcher fairies left this realm for home, we three did not want to go just yet. So after about one hundred years of wandering around in forests, we stumbled upon Darius. He was picking herbs from the forest floor for his magic. He is a great wizard, although you would call him a healer. For that is what he is," said Whisper as Derek, Kadunks, and the other fairies listened.

"He asked us what we were doing out in the forest, for he had thought that we had all passed from this world. We told him our excuse, and he said that he would give us a place to stay and live if only to do one favor of his choosing. We accepted," said Wolly.

"Since then, we have lived with Darius in a small house he made with his magic. He asked us what we would like in it before he was finished. We each told the specifications, and he had, of course, finished it to our liking. For my room, I wanted everything to be silver. That is my color, you see; every fairy has one color they favor above all others. We also have our own element, but some fairies share this element, for there are only four—water, fire, earth, and wind. Mine is water," Crystal said with a sweet smile.

"Mine is red, as is almost everything in my room as well. Whisper and Crystal call me a hot head sometimes. That name has two meanings, one for being a 'hot head' and the other is that I can control fire. I am also a prankster, which is another reason I am red. As Whisper told you before, we fairies are so small that we can hold just one emotion at a time. The emotion that we hold can be shown by the color we are. Blue is sad or scared, red is anger or mischief, pink is love or embarrassment, and so on. I love to make jokes on people; that is why I am mostly red all the time," Wolly said as he flew up and landed on Derek's shoulder.

"Derek, do you really know why you are here?" Derek seemed a little taken back by the question. But then he realized that he only knew some parts of it. The

Ashton twins told what they could, but he felt that there was something missing.

"I only know what has been told to me. I know I am here to become king, and I know of a princess locked away somewhere that I have to release," he said to Wolly, the fairy nodding.

"That is what you are to do as well. But there is more to the picture than you realize. You see there is a queen whose name is Natheria; she is the second daughter of the old king. The first daughter was heir to the throne and married at a young age and then gave birth to her heir, Princess Arria. Natheria could not handle the thought of her sister being in control and she told her father this many times. But he told her it was just meant to be. Natheria became enraged and killed her father, sister, and her sister's husband. But when she came on to Arria, the princess was not there," said Wolly. His face was serious and his color had dimmed to a calm blue.

"What do you mean the princess wasn't there?" said Zenchen wildly as he looked to the young-looking wizard for answers.

"You forget, Zenchen, the queen herself said that she had taken care of the princess. That was all she said but the people's imagination ran away with them and soon everyone thought to believe that the queen had her locked up in some cold, dark dungeon until her last dying days. But this is not true. As I told you before we left on this journey, Princess Arria has a giant spider looking out for her." Darius turned and looked at Wolly and the other fairies.

"Yes, I remember now an old legend about a great old creature that came because he had heard, like we did, that Natheria was up to something. This creature was fond of Princess Arria and would do anything to protect her. This creature is known to all fairy-like creatures, as The Guardian. I am afraid that is all that we know of it." Zenchen, the twins, and Kadunks mouths closed, shutting off the questions they were going to ask.

"We can tell you the person who is destined to go up against this creature is amongst us. It is you, Derek; you must go up against this creature in a battle of wits. If you win, you get past it; if not, you will be the same as those who have come before you," said Whisper.

"What happened to them?" asked Derek, his heart in his throat.

"They were eaten," whispered Crystal. Derek's eyes widened at the thought. He turned to his grandfather then, as if some light bulb had been clicked on, Derek jumped up looking very horrified. The others became very tense, looking around at what had made Derek act that way.

"What about me?" whispered Derek. "Just because I have to go against that thing doesn't mean I am supposed to rescue the princess, right? What if I can't or it's not me? I'll be killed, or worse, eaten." Darius got up and made his way over to a very unstable Derek. As he went, he changed his appearance to an older gentleman. He placed his hands on Derek's shoulders, making Derek look up at him. At first, there was confusion then acceptance.

"You won't be killed or eaten because you are the chosen one." Darius reached down and touched the diamond half-heart on the necklace. "This here proves that you are. Only the future husband of Princes Arria could have been born with this. I guess you could call it a birth mark." Derek calmed down and soon after, everything began to dwindle down. After that, they all continued planning what to do next. They gathered all of the supplies they needed for their upcoming journey. By the time they were all finished it was dusk, and everyone headed to their huts to retire once again.

Dream

Derek followed his grandfather into the little hut. Derek watched as the young old man moseyed about in the hut. The old wizard, Derek noticed, had changed his appearance again. He was not young as Derek anymore, but instead looked about thirty. The young boy saw some similarities in his grandfather's face that matched his own.

Before the old wizard could see Derek stare at him, Derek walked calmly into the hut. Darius looked up and smiled at him, which the young man returned. Derek went over to the bed that was not being used and sat down. He removed his boots and shirt, lay down, and pulled the covers up to his chin. He lay there for a while thinking about the vision he had seen when he had gotten his necklace.

Derek was trying to remember, for he knew that he and the princess had more talks than just that one. As he searched his brain, he slowly began to fall asleep. His eyes began to droop and Derek fought it off, but he did not last. In a matter of minutes, Derek was fast asleep.

"Hello again," said a feminine voice. Derek looked around but could not see anyone.

"Hello," he said back and there it was, a little blur of light just off to the right of where he was. He could hear giggling coming from it. It sounded like there were two people talking and laughing. As he crept closer, he could see the shadow outline of two children playing. But he could also see a wall between them. They could not touch but that did not matter to them, for they seemed to be having fun.

He crept closer because he could not hear what was being said. Suddenly, he stopped. He had come close enough to see who these children were. It was the little girl, Arria, and himself. He remembered now; he was teaching Arria how to play tic-tac-toe. That was really fun and she was having a blast. He remembered how she was going to teach it to her body guard, Ri. A sudden thought came into his head; this bodyguard of Arria's was the same monster that Darius was talking about earlier. He remembered as well that Arria had told him Ri's true name.

It was . . . darn! He could not remember what she had said. But he knew as he looked back at the children playing that she had told him the name then. But he could not hear the voices clearly enough. He watched as his little self asked a question. He could see his lips forming into "What is Ri short for?" Derek quickly looked at Arria. Her lips were moving as well into, "It is short for . . ." *No, I did not get that.* Derek wanted to go back and look again but it was not so. What was going on? He had to hear what Arria said. That was the key; you had to call the beast by his true name. But with that thought, Derek noticed that the children were fading away and that he was waking up.

"Derek," he heard. He felt someone put their hand on his shoulder and shake him. "Derek, come on little one; you must get up."

"Hmm . . ." Derek rolled over and opened his eyes to see Zenchen standing over him with a smile on his face. "What?" he asked.

"Get up, Derek, we leave out soon," Zenchen said.

And with that, he saw the redhead turn and leave the hut. Derek kicked his feet over the side and put on his shoes. He scratched his head, making his bed head worse than it was. Then it hit him like a ton of bricks. Derek's eyes opened wide and he was fully awake. "Oh!" he said and he ran outside in a hurry to find Darius. He saw the old wizard by the rest of the group. Yo, Yang, and Zenchen had packs on their backs. Kadunks had a small one in which he was playing with the strap and looking up at his father, who he wanted to impersonate. Derek would have smiled if he wasn't in such a hurry.

"Darius!" he yelled. The group turned ready for action, for Derek's voice had a sense of urgency to it. When they just saw him running over as fast as he could, they began to wonder what was wrong.

"Derek, what in the blazes . . . what's wrong?" asked Yo.

"Nothing's wrong, well, there *is* something but that is with me though, not you. But listen to this. I had a dream, well, more like a vision last night. I saw my younger self talking with Arria again. I knew this because I remember teaching her how to play tic-tac-toe. But anyway, the beast you were talking about and how nobody has ever gotten past it, well, I know the way," Derek said as fast as he could. The entire group besides Kadunks had their mouths wide open in shock.

"Wait a minute, Derek, you mean you know how to get past that beast?" asked Zenchen.

"Yes, but that's the frustrating part. You see, I can't remember what Arria said," Derek said with a bit of frustration, confusing the others.

"What do you mean, Derek?" asked the wizard. "Can you tell exactly what went on between the princess and yourself?"

"Okay I saw myself playing a game with Arria and she said, 'I have to teach this to Ri.' I asked her what Ri was short for. In the dream state I was in, I could not hear her answer but I do remember her telling me in order to get past Ri, you have to say his real name."

"That's all? I thought it was more than that," said Yo, who was a bit disappointed.

"Oh but if you get it wrong, then you fight for your life," Derek said with a smile.

A Cave

When Derek was through, he went and got the rest of his bags from the hut he was staying in. He met back up with the group a few minutes later.

"Everyone have everything? Good, because we cannot come back through this way," said Darius as he looked at everyone. Kadunks walked over to Derek and took his hand in his little one and smiled up to him. Derek smiled back. Yo and Kendal shared amused looks at the adoration Kadunks had on Derek.

"So where are we headed?" Derek asked, for he had missed the meeting.

"For now, we head to the cave in the Zonthor Mountains. We will be able to go through them that way. As for the other side, I do not know anymore; other than it is a swamp or a moor, if you would call it that. There have been rumors around that people have seen creatures in the moor, but that has yet been a fact. From there, we need to find the princess by any means possible," said the high wizard.

Hours passed as they walked through the forest. No one had said much after leaving the Keeve village.

Derek was admiring the scenery when he bumped into Yang, who had stopped in front of him.

"Okay, Derek?" Yang asked as he turned around to make sure Derek was okay from the hit.

"I'm okay but why did we stop? Are we there yet?" he asked while adjusting his pack.

"Yes. We will camp here tonight and then in the morning we will find the cave. It has been many years since I have been here and the foliage has changed much," said Darius. The group dropped packs and began bustling around for provisions for the camp.

"Derek can you go and get some fire wood?" asked Yo.

Derek nodded and set off. He stopped though when he heard Kadunks. "Momma can I go with him?" the child asked.

"Yes you may, but stay closer to Derek and don't wander off; this place is not like the forest at home," answered Kendal, who was helping her husband set up a tent for her family. Kadunks smiled and took off at a run straight toward Derek. Whisper and Wolly decided to tag along. As the little company was busy looking for firewood, Derek stumbled onto a cave of pure blackness. Taken by surprise, Derek stumbled backwards onto his rump. "Oomph!" he grunted as he landed.

"Derek?" asked Whisper, his voice filled with concern.

"Huh?"

Kadunks turned and made his way back toward where he had seen Derek, only to find him on the ground. "Derek?" he cried.

"I'm fine, Kadunks, but can you go get Darius and the others for me please?" Kadunks nodded and set out for the camp. When Kadunks was gone, Derek looked back at the cave; there was something about the cave that set him off. As he turned his head listening for the others, he heard a scraping noise coming from the cave. Derek turned and peered into the blackness. Not seeing anything, he wondered if his imagination was playing tricks on him. He shook his head and turned to continue to watch for the others. "Eeehh!" Derek's head whipped around so fast you would think he got whiplash.

"Wha . . .?" he heard Whisper say. Both of their eyes were wide with fear of the unknown sound that he had heard. Derek kept his eyes glued on the entrance to the cave; there, a small movement was seen. Derek's breathing was going out of control with panic. "Eeehh!" the sound erupted once again, but this time a creature leapt out of the cave at Derek. "Aaaaaahhhh!" Derek screamed as he saw this thing run toward him. Derek turned and ran but did not get very far because the creature's arm swiped out and hit him in the side, knocking him against a tree.

"Derek!" Whisper screamed, his body changing into several of colors. Whisper started to zoom around the creature to distract it from Derek. He was shooting off small flares of lighting at it. "Eeehh!" The thing swung its mandible-like arms around. Whisper was flying and zigzagging around, trying to miss the large arms.

Derek saw lights dance around his eyes as he tried to get his bearings back; he saw the creature was about to take another swing at him. He rolled to his right to avoid the swipe of death. "Eeehh!" the creature screamed again, but it did not sound like the previous ones. Derek tuned to see arrows protruding out of the chest of the thing.

"Derek, are you all right?" asked someone Derek could not see who. He saw the twins both armed with their bows pulled back and letting arrows fly into the creature. Darius and the other two fairies joined Whisper in the throwing of spells. Wolly was firing off flares of fire, while Crystal was shooting off waves of ice at its feet, trying to get it off balance. Derek saw Zenchen running around to the back of the thing. He jumped up and swung with all his might and swished his blade cut right through the creature's head, knocking it off. It fell to the ground, twitching every minute or so.

"Derek!" a frightened voice called. He turned to see Kadunks running toward him with tears running down his face. "Derek!" The others ran toward him. Yo helped him off the ground and was starting to check him over. Derek then noticed he felt something warm and wet running down the side of his face and neck. He placed a hand there and it came back covered in blood.

"It's all right," he heard Yo say. "You just scratched yourself when you hit the tree. Head wounds always bleed more." Derek heard ripping sounds and saw Yo and Yang were ripping an old shirt into small ribbons. They tied them around Derek's head to stop the bleeding.

"What was that thing?" he asked as he looked at the creature.

"I have no idea. I have never heard or seen such a thing in my life. What about you, Darius?" Yo asked.

"No, neither have I." Derek walked over to thing that came out of the cave. He was shocked at what he saw. The creature looked like a praying mantis–human hybrid. It was humanoid but with green skin, long legs that bended the opposite way, and had spikes coming out of the back of them. The arms of the mantis were exactly like that of one—claws instead of hands. The head was that of a human but its mouth, which was hanging wide open, was layered with sharp teeth. It looked like there were at least three layers of teeth. Derek shuddered at the prospect of being eaten by this thing.

"I found the cave you were looking for, Grandpa," Derek said in a small voice. "This thing came out of it and attacked me," Derek said as he pointed to a point in the bushes. Darius walked forward to where Derek was pointing and went past the foliage. A few seconds later, he remerged.

"It is indeed the cave, but we do not yet know if there are any more of those things in there or not. For now, we go back to the campsite and set up a perimeter. We will set out before sunrise and we will get through the cave by late tomorrow, if we do not have any more interruptions like that," Darius said as he led Derek back to camp.

A Long, Dark Walk

The first person out of the group that woke up was Whisper; he had snuggled against Derek's head during the night and now as he looked around him, he wondered why he did not get squashed during the night. He was sitting right in-between Derek's head and Kadunks's, who undoubtedly crawled into their tent to be with Derek. The young fairy smiled, for he knew that the young half-cat had looked at Derek as an older brother.

Whisper then got up, flew to the entrance of the tent, and put his shoes back on. He then flew through one of the gaping holes in the entrance and left the camp to find water. Whisper flew for a few moments until he came upon the small stream he had seen yesterday, and landed near the bank. Leaning over he washed the sleep from his eyes. Not long after he was joined by Wolly and Crystal.

Back at the camp, Derek opened his eyes groggily, rolled over, and grabbed the nearest thing he could snuggle onto. That thing made a sound that sounded like a high-pitched grunt. He thought, *That's not right;*

"What is so funny all of the sudden, huh?" asked Darius.

"It's funny that every time you call Derek 'Grandson' or he calls you 'Granddad or Grandfather,' you get all starry eyed and begin saying, 'how I love it when you say that.' It is simply hilarious," said Yo.

"Hrmp, I am simply happy that I have my grandchild near me, is that so wrong?" Darius said with a fake sad voice. The others broke out into laughter again and Kadunks joined in not knowing what was so funny, but he joined in because his daddy was laughing. Derek started laughing as well at Kadunks, as well as at his grandfather.

It wasn't soon after everyone stopped laughing that Derek noticed the walls of the cave began to get lighter in color.

"We are at the end of the cave, everyone. We made it safe and sound and with a little more daylight than I thought we would have," Darius announced. Everyone was walking faster to get to the exit. Soon everyone was running trying to get out of the cave. Derek gave a great sigh of relief as he exited the cave and he took in a deep breath of cool, fresh air.

Who Was That?
What Is This?

Derek opened his eyes, for he smelled something that was different. It was not a bad smell but not good either. It smelled wet and of mud; he looked around and saw that it was indeed mud. Lots of it by the looks of things. Darius was right; it was a moor. Derek racked his brain; moors meant mud and mud meant quicksand.

"Hey, listen up. I have just thought of something very important and I want all of you to know about it; it could mean the difference between life and death," Derek said, and he saw that he had all of their attention.

"I just remembered something about moors. When I was in my world, I had this book that was all about moors and in it, it said that moors have deep places in it that you can get caught in and never get out of. Those places are called quicksand. If you fall in one, it basically sucks you in and the more you fight the faster you get sucked in." He saw everyone's faces go white.

"That is indeed information to know about, Derek, thank you. But do you know if we can point out such places?" he asked his grandson.

"Well, in the book it said that sometimes the patches of quicksand look lighter than the ground next to it. But like I said, that's only sometimes; other times you won't know it is there until you step in it. I suggest we all find a long stick so we can probe the ground around us so we don't fall in one," suggested Derek as he looked around for such a thing. Everyone nodded and began looking for such a stick.

"Okay we have just about everything we need to cross the moor on foot. Let's pull out the tents and set up camp here for the night and continue on tomorrow," advised Darius. Derek, who was lying in his tent long after everyone had fallen asleep, could not seem to find sleep himself. He was thinking about all that had happened to him so far and of the dream he had before they left the Keeve village when he heard a splash.

He sat up and looked at Kadunks who was with him to see if he woke up. Derek smiled a bit seeing Kadunks sleeping so soundly, but he turned his attention now on the splashing sounds coming not far from them.

He got up and put on his boots and crawled out of his tent. He moved slowly and picked up his stick he had placed near his tent. He probed his way toward the splashing sounds. Then he happened upon it; it was a small watering pool big enough to swim in. Derek's attention was soon drawn upon the figure in the pool. He ventured toward it a little more to get a better look.

Derek blinked not believing what his eyes were showing him. It looked like a girl but from the moonlight it seemed her skin was dark brown. She looked human enough if you didn't count the wings she had coming from behind her. They looked like the wings you would find on a wasp or bee.

They were beautiful, shining in the moonlight. Derek moved forward again trying to get a better look than the one he had. *Click.* He had stepped on a twig; he looked up to see the girl looking in his direction and she shot out and ran so fast he had trouble following her. He sighed and turned to go back to his tent. He crawled in after removing his boots and fell instantly asleep, his dreams filled with girls with wasp wings.

Derek was shaken awake by Kadunks. He nodded his head and got up for the coming day. He stopped what he was doing because he caught the whiff of something fowl. Derek smelled himself and let out an "ugh" sound and thought to himself he would tell everyone about the glade pool and wash up before moving on. He exited his tent ad walked over to his grandfather.

"Granddad," he said.

"Yes," Darius answered.

"I found something last night after everyone was asleep. I heard a splashing sound coming from over there and so I followed it. I took my stick," he said as he saw his grandfather's face, "and went to find it. I found a small glade pool where we can wash off because I know I smell pretty bad. But I saw something in the pool when I found it. It looked like a girl with really dark skin, but what was amazing was she had wings like a bee's on her back," Derek said.

"Really? That is some news; did you get to talk to her any?" asked Zenchen.

"No, I stepped on a stick and she ran off and man was she fast. I didn't even see her move and then poof she was gone."

Wolly whistled.

"Well, we can't do much about that but we can find this pool and get more drinking water. Derek, can you lead the way?" asked Darius. Derek nodded and everyone got everything packed up and Derek led the way to the glade.

He found it soon enough and everyone got cleaned up as best they could, and stocked up on drinking water. Soon they found themselves back at the cave.

"Okay I don't know this terrain very much but I do know the queen's castle is way up northwest from here. We don't want to go there, so we have the option of either going straight or southwest, which way do you all want to go?" asked Darius.

"Wait Darius, you don't have to do that. We know the princess is southwest; we can feel the power of The Guardian that way. He would not be very far from the princess," said Whisper.

Darius nodded his head. "Okay, now we have our heading; let's move out." Darius turned and was just about to take a step into the moor when all of the sudden four creatures sprang out of the mud in front of them.

"Who are you and what business do you have on our moor?"

Breinigsville, PA USA
03 February 2011
254659BV00002BA/8/P